The Yoga Ogre

For Tara
PB

For Erin and Isla
SR

SIMON AND SCHUSTER

First published in Great Britain in 2012 by Simon and Schuster UK Ltd • 1st Floor, 222 Gray's Inn Road, London WC1X 8HB • A CBS Company

Text copyright © 2012 Peter Bently • Illustrations copyright © 2012 Simon Rickerty • The right of Peter Bently and Simon Rickerty to be identified as

the author and illustrator of this work has been asserted by them in accordance with the Copyright, Designs and Patents Act, 1988 • All rights reserved,

including the right of reproduction in whole or in part in any form • A CIP catalogue record for this book is available from the British Library upon request

ISBN: 978-1-84738-902-2 (HB) 978-1-84738-903-9 (PB) • Printed in China • 10 9 8 7 6 5 4 3 2 1

The Yoga Ogre

by Peter Bently
and Simon Rickerty

SIMON AND SCHUSTER
London   New York   Sydney   Toronto   New Delhi

Ogden the Ogre was worried one night.
His jim-jams had grown far too short and too tight!

"How has my tum got so terribly wide?
I only eat TWELVE meals a day," Ogden sighed.

The people said, "Jim-jams too tight and too short?
Overweight ogres should take up a sport!"

... as he slam-dunked the roof off the church and the steeple.

Then Ogden tried football.

The people cried,
"STOP!"...

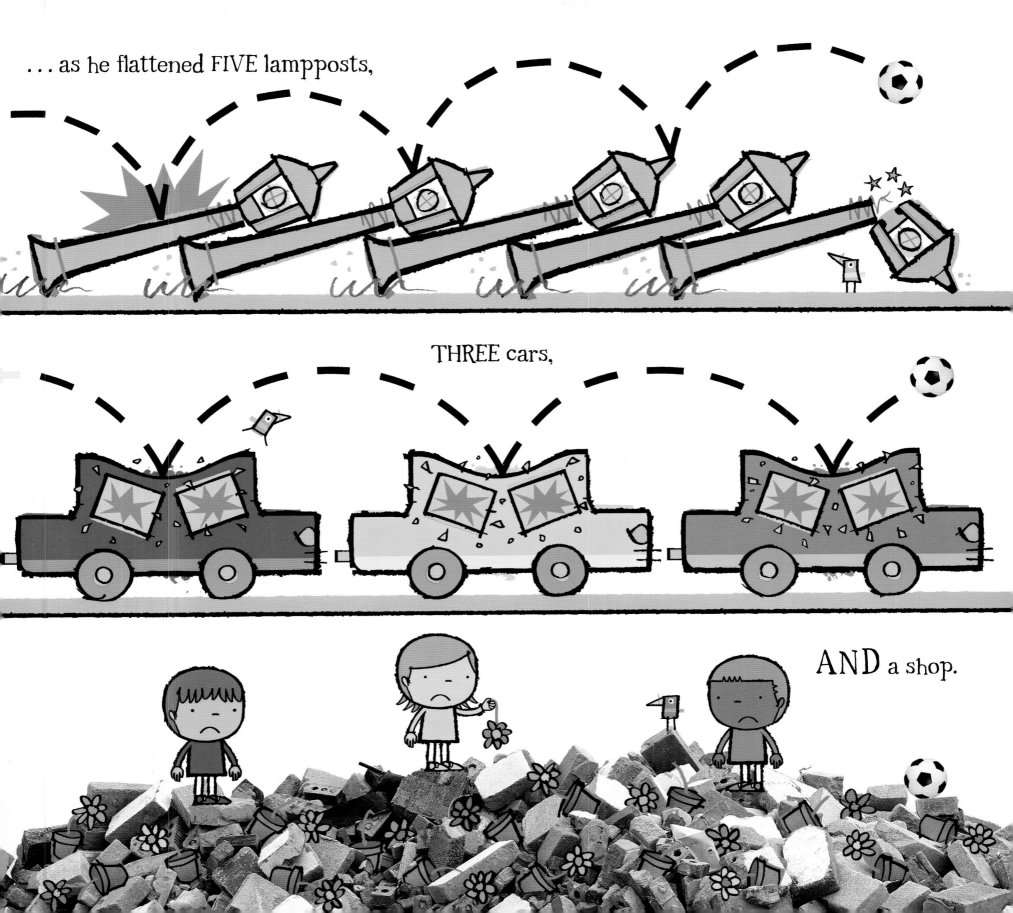

The people took shelter when Ogden tried hockey.

And the horses all hid when
he dressed as a jockey!

He gave up on golf at the very first tee.

There's now a HUGE hole where the course used to be!

The people said, "Want to be slim as a wafer?
Why not try yoga? It's really much safer."

"Yoga?" thought Ogden. "You folks could be right.
I'll try the new class at the town hall tonight!"

"First," said the teacher, "lie down on the floor."

"Now twist your leg over . . ."

ker-RASH *went the door.*

"Let's stand on one leg like a tree, straight and tall."

WOBBLE went Ogden . . .

"Being upside down is a really good feeling.
Let's try a handstand ..."

"Enough is enough!" cried the people. "By heck!
Our nerves are in shreds and the town hall's a wreck.

It's simply a menace when ogres play sport.
Please give up ball games of EVERY sort!"

"And also," they said, "will you please understand
that yoga is totally, utterly, BANNED!"

"I do understand," sighed the sorrowful ogre.
"I'll stop playing sports and I'll stop doing yoga."

"I'll have to find some other way to get thinner.
Perhaps I could only have TEN pies for dinner!"

Next morning the town was remarkably quiet.
The people thought, "Great! Ogden's gone on a diet!"

"How peaceful it is with no ogre in sight!
How pleasant! How tranquil!" they sighed in delight.

But . . .

then came a thunderous thudding
and thumping.
A shuddering,
juddering stumping
and bumping.
The people thought,
"Heavens! Whatever is making
that booming and banging,
that shaking and quaking?"

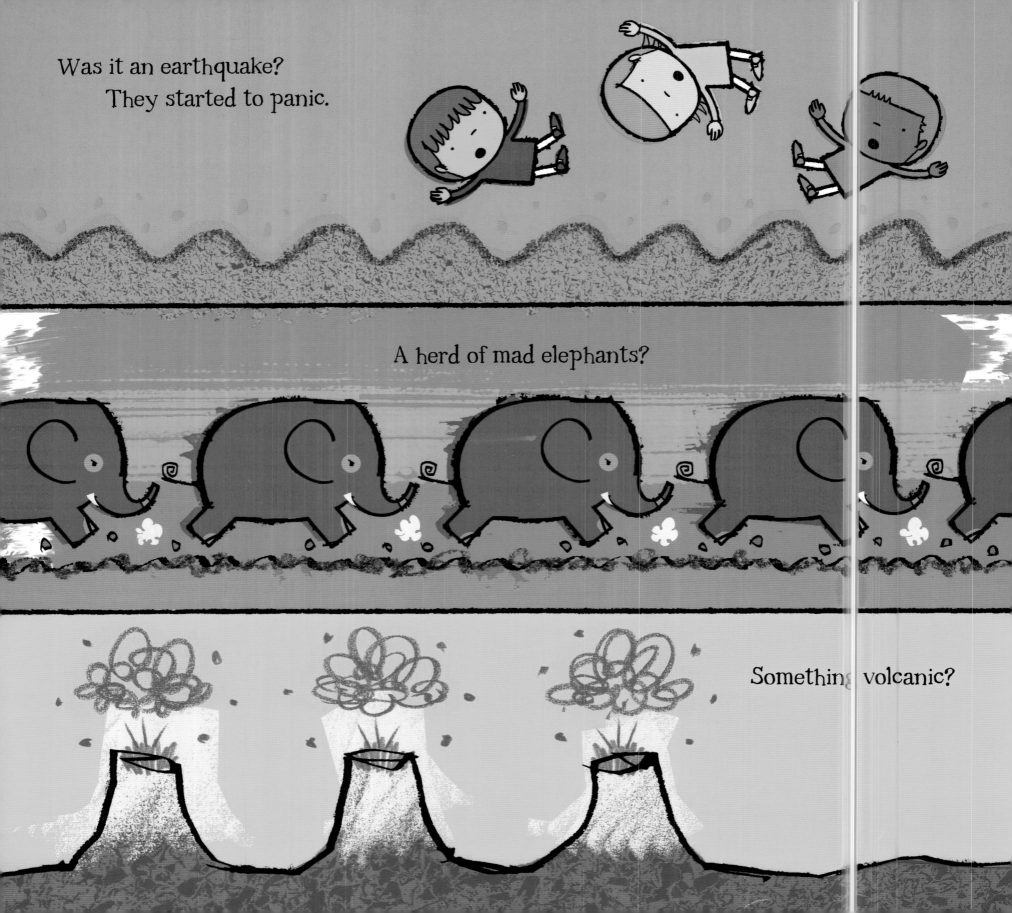

Was it an earthquake?
They started to panic.

A herd of mad elephants?

Something volcanic?

"Oh, no!"

cried the people in terror and dread . . .

"Ogden has taken up jogging instead!"

THE END.